LOLLY'S BASEMENT CRAWLIES

by Cynthia Soda

AuthorHouse™
1663 Liberty Drive
Bloomington, IN 47403
www.authorhouse.com
Phone: 1-800-839-8640

First published by AuthorHouse   04/14/2011

ISBN: 978-1-4567-4562-2 (sc)

Library of Congress Control Number: 2011903600

Printed in the United States of America

Any people depicted in stock imagery provided by Thinkstock are models,
and such images are being used for illustrative purposes only.
Certain stock imagery © Thinkstock.

This book is printed on acid-free paper.

authorHOUSE®

Dedication:

To my family; especially Matt, my love; Sofia, my princess and for my baby sister Kassandra... thank you for being my basement buddy and protecting your big cowardly sister from the Boogey Monster.

Lolly had just sat down to watch her favourite episode of Bernie Big Bear on TV when she heard her mom call from the kitchen:

"Lolly!! Honey, can you please go down to the basement to get some bread in the fridge for me?"

"Can't Peter do it, Mommy?" she asked in her sweetest princess voice. She didn't want to admit how scared she was of the basement.

"Your brother's doing his homework right now, *please* sweetie?" asked her mom.

So Lolly got off her comfy spot on the couch, left her favourite TV show, and huffed and puffed her way to the basement door. She stood looking at the menacing doorknob, took a deep breath and *slowly* opened the door... "CREEEEEAK" screeched the door.

Lolly's heart began to beat faster and faster and faster. Her hands got cold and sweaty. She started to think about all the creepy crawlies, stinky rats, slithery snakes and worst of all... the Boogey Monster! All of them were hiding behind the door just *waiting* for Lolly to make her first move down the creaky steps... she just *knew* it.

Taking a deep breath, Lolly flung the door wide open and flicked the light on. She walked slowly down the stairs, careful not to make too much noise because she didn't want to wake the basement creatures. Lolly slowly turned the corner when she saw something hiding in the darkness...

"We've been *waiting* for you." Said the Boogey Monster, and he grinned so she could see his mouthful of big sharp teeth.

"Um.. I.. I just have to get some bread.. and... umm.. then my Mommy needs me upstairs." Lolly almost peed her pants! She was never ready to see the Boogey Monster, no matter how hard she tried to prepare herself for him. She hesitantly backed away from the monster, turned the corner and switched the lights on, when all of a sudden...

"SURPRISE!" All the creepy crawlies, stinky rats and slithery snakes jumped out from behind the couch and they were all holding *presents*! Even the Boogey Monster joined in! In the middle of the room was Lolly's favourite kind of cake, a super-dooper-triple fudge-chocolate cream-cookie cake!

"AHHHHHHH!" Screamed Lolly.

"AHHHHHHH!" Screamed the creatures and they accidentally knocked the super-dooper-triple fudge-chocolate cream-cookie cake onto the floor. Lolly slipped on it, and she went sliding through the basement crawlies knocking them down like bowling pins! Presents went flying, ribbons were tangling and monsters were crashing! Lolly ended up at the bottom of a huge monster pile-up!

"Let me out of here!" Lolly demanded.

"We just wanted to wish you a happy b-b-birthday." they cried.

"Well it's not my birthday!" she said, and with that she got up and brushed the dust off her clothes. "You guys drive me CRAZY! I never want to come down here because I'm afraid that you'll all scare me!" she huffed.

The monsters looked at each other, confused.

"Now I'm going to get some bread for my Mommy and go upstairs, and you guys are all going to leave me alone!"

The monsters began to cry. "Please don't leave us, Lolly! We're so *lonely* down here by ourselves!" So Lolly huffed and puffed some more before deciding to stay a little while longer. Maybe the basement crawlies weren't so scary after all... they just wanted to be friends. The monsters cheered and played some music while they all sang and danced. Then they sat down to watch "Monster and the Malt Factory" on the big TV.

"Oh no! Look at the time!" said Lolly after the movie, "I have to bring bread up to my Mommy! She's going to be SO ANGRY!" She jumped up off the couch and grabbed the bread out of the fridge. She said good-bye to her new friends and raced up the stairs.

"Here's the bread, Mommy!" Lolly smiled and used her sweetest princess voice.

"Lolly Sofia Lupini!" said her mom using her full name.. *that* meant she was in trouble.. "YOU ARE AN ABSOLUTE MESS! What were you *doing* down there, *making* the bread?"

"Well..." said Lolly "not *exactly*..."

THE END

About the Author

Cynthia Soda is a Canadian-born artist and interior designer. She grew up in a small town north of Toronto and graduated from Ryerson University School of Interior Design. *Lolly's Basement Crawlies* was inspired by her own fear of the basement growing up. The story is meant to show children (and adults!) that sometimes the unknown isn't as scary as you think!

Cynthia currently works and lives in her hometown with her husband and baby girl. This is her first children's story.